Cora & The Power of Five

Rhae'nell Allen

Exhale Publishing

Published in 2021 by Rhae'nell Allen with help of Exhale Publishing

Copyright © Rhae'nell Allen

Exhale Publishing is part of 4D-House Ltd.

4D HOUSE

Prepared for publishing by Careen Latoya Lawrence
Editor: Careen Latoya Lawrence
Illustrator: M.I.Designs

A CIP catalogue record for this title is available from the British Library.

Acknowledgements

To all my readers, you are just like Cora; A superhero in your own right. Just remember not all heroes wear capes or suits!

First of all, I would want to thank my parents for loving and supporting me and for encouraging me to go for my dreams. They took me seriously when I told them I wanted to become an author and supplied me with an endless amount of books. I'm a bookworm.

When I was 4-years old, I wrote a poem that my big cousin read and from that day she was confident that I will grow up to be a writer and that she would support and encourage me every step of the way. So, for that reason, I would like to reserve a special acknowledgement to Careen Latoya Lawrence for instilling the belief that I can become an author and for the support, she has provided to help me achieve one of my dreams.

This leads me to my next thank you, which goes to the fantastic team at 4D-House Limited. They have worked hard with my parents and me in turning my 13,000+ word document into a physical, colourful published book that I'm delighted you the reader have in your hands now.

Thank you all for your patience and attention to detail. I literally couldn't have done this without you!

Thank you to all my family and friends. There are far too many to list you all, but I love you all equally and dearly. Though I tried to keep this a surprise from them in the earlier stages, they still always showed love, support, and, encouragement for a *'certain project' that I'm working on,* they always wanted the best for me.

I would also like to thank a memorable person from my childhood that also counts as a role model for me; my exceptionally great childminder Aunty Nett. She is an amazing person to look up to and I learned so much from her at a very young age. Thanks Aunty Nett for the skills you taught me. And last but by no means least a MASSIVE thank you goes to you the reader! I'm still pinching myself. This is a real book.

My book!

It doesn't feel as though much time has passed from the days when all my 'books' were held together with a stapler, or laid out in pencil in my sparkly notebooks.

I hope enjoy you!

No Ordinary Family

Hi, I'm Cora Martin. I have a little sister called Coco and an older brother named Cameron, who can be annoying and rude, but he loves us deep down, I think.

I'm thirteen, Cameron is sixteen, Coco is seven, and our golden retriever, Lucky is around two. Coco goes to the primary school next to me; our playgrounds are next to each other so I see her during the day. She is always bullied because of how smart she is. She does our taxes! Brilliant, right? Especially for our parents.

Cameron is smart too, but he doesn't use his smarts for good. He is ALWAYS pranking someone, whether it's hacking the fire alarm system, making the alarms go off, or changing students' grades on their permanent record; either as a favour or for revenge, depending on his mood. For whatever the reason, he's still popular and one of the coolest kids in school. Then you have me, the dorky one in the school choir who never gets noticed by our teacher, Madam Lyntoinette. I always felt like the one who never got the good end. Even the names.

A name like Cameron just sounds like it's made for the famous and Coco is tremendously exotic. Then you have Cora. Just Cora. Not saying that your name is bad if it is Cora. It's just that I don't have a good thing going for me. I mean, why couldn't I be Catalina? Or Cadance? Or Ceciliana? Or Clairice? Or anything else? Anyway, back to my story. I felt like a weak link for most of my life.

Even compared to my parents, my dad is a scientist, and my mum is an animal trainer. But my best friend Stephanie has always treated me like I was special, however, I never believed her until one very bizarre day.

It was a perfect morning because it was the last day of school before the summer holiday. In fact, the entire day was perfect, well, it was until home time.

I eagerly packed my bag with my books and lazily slung it over my shoulder and headed out of class. Walking casually through the hallway, I was laughing at Stephanie, who was doing an uncanny impression of an angry Professor Spencer. That's when the stereotypical 'cool kids' sauntered to their lockers which was right next to ours.

I had been trying to get into their clique for AGES and no matter what I do, it seems as if I'm always invisible to them. You have Winter, the leader, and she has a heart like her name. Well, she acts like it. Next up is Alfred, he has a sharp fashion sense and a flare for gossip. Lastly, there is Georgia, she has more trophies for rhythmic gymnastics than you could ever imagine.

"Go over to them." Stephanie insisted, shoving me towards them.

I started off in their direction but as I got halfway down the hall, I hesitated, turning to look desperately at Stephanie who gave me an encouraging nod. I took the deepest breath ever and spun on my heels and continued in the direction of the cool ones.

I tapped Winter on the shoulder and shuffled my feet when she turned to look at me. She seemed to grow a dozen feet tall, while I felt like I was shrinking towards the ground. She put a hand on her hip as the others turned and did the same.

"You're really cool and I think we should be friends. No. Best friends. No. Roommates. No. ADOPT ME!

"Wait, that was wrong. Want to hang out at gym class?

"YOLO. RIP. IDK. FOMO. HASHTAG. OMG.

"Sorry, I babble when I'm nervous-

"Did I just say that?

"STUPID! STUPID! STUPID!

"I really want to be your friend."

To say I rambled, would be a huge understatement! The entire school seemed to be laughing at me and my cheeks burned. I swivelled on my heel and bolted out of the hall and into the bathroom. I slammed the door to a cubicle and locked myself in as I started to sob. A few seconds later, the door swung open and a concerned Stephanie jogged in.

"Cora? Cora? CORA MARTIN! CORA GWYNETH MARTIN! WHERE ARE YOU?" She yelled.

"Hey, you promised to not use my middle name." I sniffed.

"AHA!" She triumphed. "Wait, where are you?"

"I'm here. In the end cubicle..." I replied, sticking my foot out from under the door. "Can't you see my shoes?"

"NO YOU'RE NOT!" She huffed. "STOP MESSING ABOUT!" She yelled.

"I'm NOT! Look!" I shouted back, pushing the door open and throwing a tissue at her. I slammed it shut again.

"There! I SAW IT! WHAT ON EARTH IS HAPPENING?" She screamed.

"Never mind that, what I want to know, is how you found me so quickly." I cut in through her breakdown.

"I know you." She answered. "Besides, where else do girls go when they're upset at school?"

I couldn't help but giggle at her and I suddenly felt a pang of love and appreciation for her. I really don't deserve Stephanie.

"Oh gosh not you." She grumbled. "Sorry, I mean; hello."

"WHAT?" I cried.

"Someone's here to see you." She whispered.

I looked through the bottom of the cubicle to see a small pair of shiny black Kickin' Kiddies, size 1 school shoes, a pair of Louboutins and particularly scaly claws. I groaned at the thought of who it was.

"Cora darling, come out dear." Called a shrill voice.

It was my one and only aunt June. She is so extra. By this point she was pounding on the door.

I opened the door and waited for some sort of reaction as I stepped out.

"Cora?" They asked, turning their heads, searching for me, while I was still standing right there, staring at my Aunt's peacock.

Yes, she has a peacock. A hassling, female peacock, my aunt, Stephanie and Coco. Coco stumbled into me, causing a domino effect.

My aunt's peacock, called Pearl, toppled over, then Aunt June then Stephanie. We were a crumpled heap on the floor.

To see if they were playing a joke, I jumped up and looked in the mirror. Horrified at not being able to see my face, I let out a loud howl trying to unscramble my brain.

"I don't get it. I'm here but nobody can see me." I sighed.

Aunt June gasped. She stood up and opened her mouth to say something but quickly closed it again.

She thought better of it and dragged Coco away with Pearl strutting at their side. Stephanie's face was drained of all colour and frozen with shock.

"Are you ok?" I asked, trying to push confidence into my voice. All she did was point at me and stutter.

I went back to the mirror where I could finally see myself and I shook Stephanie so much that it somehow brought life back to her. She jumped up and we wondered the same thing, what on Earth could be happening?

She took my hand and led me to the car park, making rude gestures at people who mocked me along the way. When we got to the car park, I saw an elaborate pink Lamborghini parked, waiting for me. This could only mean one thing, aunt June.

I hugged Stephanie, unable to resist sniffing her glossy brown hair that smelt of lavender and chestnuts before I climbed into the car.

It was an insufferable journey. Aunt June had the opera music up full blast, her little lady of a peacock, whom she decided to name Pearl because of her love for all things glitzy, was sitting on top of Coco and I. Coco had brought a revolting smelling project with her and I was stuck to my seat as aunt June swerved while applying what had to be her ninetieth coat of lipstick.

"Did you know the female peacock is called a peahen? They do not have long feathers like the males. I'm telling you this because her name is Pearl and did you know that Pearl is a name that can be used for males and females?" Aunt June informed us for the hundredth time.

"Yes aunt June, you told us before." Coco and I chorused.

"Hey, where's Cameron?" I asked, making Aunt June fume with a loud 'harrumph' Coco burst into a million fits of laughter. GET ME OUT OF THIS DEATHHOLE! I screamed internally.

After what seemed like an eternity, aunt June screeched to a stop at our destination. I opened the car door and fell out. Yes! I literally fell on the floor FACE FLAT. Grumbling about how badly I hate my life, I picked myself up and trudged indoors. I was still feeling bad about what had just happened so I ran upstairs and rapped on Cameron's door.

"What?" He called from inside.

"Just let me -" I was cut off by a gigantic golden retriever. "WOAH!" She's our pet, Lucky. Whenever I get home, she leaps on me and covers me in dog slobber. "Hi there girl." I spluttered under her licks.

Cameron's door swung open and it was no surprise to me that he was wearing his headset, holding his controller and left his room in complete darkness. He lifted Lucky off me and let us in. Coco came dashing up the stairs following us.

"What happened?" I asked Cameron, quizzing his absence in the car.

"YEAH! Tell us!" Coco interrupted.

"I knew you were in some kind of trouble when aunt June had to pick you up and you interrupted her yoga class.

She was fuming because she was the only option while dad was coming home from work!" Coco laughed.

Cameron barely flinched and carelessly explained, "All I did was pretend to hack into Mrs. Morris's email and-"

"WAIT MRS. MORRIS?" Coco and I gasped in unison, both sitting on his bed.

"Yes, the headteacher of both the schools. I sent her a fake threatening message online, saying that I would steal her school plans and her headteacher status if she didn't let us have more sweets in the vending machines and 100 day holidays with 3 day weekends. She thought that I was a serious hacker and reminded me that she could call the police. They caught me and I was sent home. Aunt June had to charm her way to get me out of serious trouble." Cameron replied proudly.

"Try not to make teachers hate me more than they already do, please. I don't need you pulling down my readily dragged name because you're my brother." I moaned.

"Yeah, I don't want my spotless reputation to be ruined!" Coco insisted.

It might have been on his permanent record, but Cameron is Cameron and if it means no school, it's a win to him. I shook my head in disbelief and just shrugged off to my room. Coco plopped down on my beanbag and tried to get me involved in her revolting Chemistry project.

I swear that child needs to skip primary school, high school AND college so she can just go to university. Her IQ is more than mum's, dad's, aunt June's, Cameron's and mine COMBINED! It's been scientifically proven. I'm serious, my parents were rattled and sent her to some science lab so she could be tested. That's when we found out that her IQ was 'incomprehensible' whatever that could mean.

What happened today rang in my head continuously, no matter how hard I tried to ignore it, there was a feeling that something was wrong.

I went along silently until dinner.

Dad called us downstairs because we always dine together, as a family. Dad came in, holding lasagne and homemade garlic dough balls. Lucky bounded in before Pearl and aunt

June as we all sat down. Dad was dishing up our food when mum hurried in. She's a wildlife biologist and often mentors up and coming zoologists, while my Dad is an archaeologist, now we know where Coco got her smarts from, and aunt June doesn't work, but is somehow a trillionaire.

"I made it just in time!" Mum chirped, she sat down with all of us staring at her. She had a bruise on her arm, a few grazes and scratches all over her and she had a huge cut on her eyebrow. Mum looked at our expressions and quickly answered, "the girl I'm mentoring dropped her mountain tiger cub and it went berserk. I'm fine though."

We stared at her expectantly and Dad held the plate away from her.

"What?" She flickered her eyes around at us.

"WASH YOUR HANDS THEN!" We all commanded. She nervously laughed and sprinted to the bathroom and back.

We resumed what we were doing and tucked in on dinner. "How was your day Coco?" Dad asked. Coco replied by exploding into a long explanation, using words that I couldn't even think of the meaning behind.

I had a strong feeling to say something about today but I suppressed it. I tried to suppress it but couldn't help it when they asked me about my day. I described what happened exactly as I explained it to you.

Mum, dad and aunt June stared at each other. Cameron and Coco turned to look at me with their eyebrows raised. Lucky and Pearl darted out of the room. Their reactions really shocked me, though I was more interested in why the adults looked as if they were expecting it someday.

"Okay, everyone can eat in their rooms. Bye June, bye Pearl." Mum jumped back into action, breaking the silence. Dad started ushering aunt June and Pearl out the door. Mum pushed my siblings up the stairs but grabbed my arm and led me to the garden.

I was mystified by the sunset but Mum snapped me back into focus.

"I'm going to explain something to you, but you can NEVER **EVER** tell anyone what I'm about to tell you. **Not even Coco and Cameron**. Now, do you promise to not say anything?" Mum whispered.

"Sure." I mumbled.

Mum took a deep breath before bursting into exposition. "Many years ago, our ancestor Arya went up against a very evil, powerful person and his horrible invention. She banished him with her very special sceptre that contained a beam of sunlight, a speck of the moon, star dust, and grass dew. Some say that it was the most powerful thing in the world. She had a group of friends to help her and a blinding light engulfed them, leaving their valuables only. The world will only be safe again when each item is brought back to their original places. The light that swallowed them gave us powers and others around. We each get it at the age of 18 usually. When we first get it, we have a haywire to show that we've controlled it and you get extra helping powers along with your main one." She explained.

I inhaled, then bolted to my room and launched onto my bed. I lay awake for hours until I finally found sleep.

Super Training

Mum woke me up at around 4:00 am the next day and told me to put my clothes on. "Muuuuum! It's midnight!" I groaned groggily, over exaggerating.

"It is exactly 4 am!" Mum beamed.

"See? Only crazy people are up at this time, like you." I whined, throwing a pillow at her. She gave me the dreaded death stare, so, I did what she said before she led me to the back garden.

"We know what your power is, invisibility, but we need to find out what's activating it," Mum said in a professional voice.

"How do we do that?" I yawned.

Mum was about to speak when our nosy neighbours, Mr. and Mrs. Wood, started arguing very loudly. I told you crazy people were up at this time. Mum spun around three times and vanished as a blue light swallowed her. I could hear her talking to them, before she reappeared while the Woods were silent. "I can teleport, and my perk is being persuasive." Mum chirped. 'Now, our task is to do different things that may have happened during the day."

First was loyalty. Mum started saying mean things about Lucky. She loved Lucky, and, we all know it, so that was a failure.

Next up was sadness. Mum took my favourite shirt and let Lucky use it as his chew toy. I snatched it back, and it was full of slobber.

"YES!" Mum cheered. "YOUR HAIR JUST DISAPPEARED!"

I squealed as I saw my hands turn invisible.

Then, we tried fear. Mum randomly ran towards me, holding the creepiest doll I've ever seen and I covered my face. "YOU'VE COMPLETELY VANISHED! Oh, no. You're visible again." Mum exclaimed.

Then we tried all sorts of things to try to figure out why. I balled my fists and grumbled, "ARRRGGGHHH!"

"So it's a frustration motivation!" She laughed.

So my superpowers were strongest with strong emotions. Little did I know that superhero training would be a nightmare.

The next few days of the summer holiday were spent learning to control my powers.

I had to ignore all my friends texting me to join their fun activities. I noticed that mum was right. It was hard, scary and I hated every waking second of my life. Stephanie would invite me somewhere, but mum forced me to stay and train though I really wanted to go.

Every day I watched as dad would take Cameron and Coco somewhere fun. Aunt June would do fun things with them and post pictures. My friends were having the time of their lives and posting pictures. It all got too much. One day, I had enough. We were trying to learn my easy move when I saw aunt June, dad, Coco and Cameron on a Cruise Ship Tour of London. Stephanie posted a picture with her entire household having a picnic.

"I'M DONE WITH THIS!" I snapped. "ALL MY FRIENDS AND FAMILY ARE HAVING FUN WHILE I'M STUCK HERE!"

I ran inside, stormed upstairs and slammed my bedroom door shut. I launched myself onto my bed and started crying into my pillow. Mum knocked on the door.

"GO AWAY!" I sniffed.

She kept knocking.

"Fine." I whimpered.

Mum opened the door.

"Sweetheart, I know that it's hard but as soon as we work out the perk and the attack you can do whatever you want with your friends." She smiled, sitting on my bed.

I didn't believe her. We would do more, and more work. We would have to save the world and my life was over! I sobbed even harder into my pillow.

"I HATE this!" I wailed.

Mum hugged me while I wept into her jumper.

Aunt June, dad, Cameron and Coco came home laughing. They had fish and chips, and we ate them outside on the bench.

"How was your dancing lesson?" Cameron asked me through a mouthful of fish.

I turned to stare at mum and she answered him for me. "She's improving a lot. So much in fact, that we're going to nationals, I'm afraid it will last all summer though. We'll hopefully win a prize or something."

Mum lied flawlessly.

I nodded as she put her arm around me and I awkwardly agreed at this complete, bold face lie.

"What kind of dance lessons are you talking about mum?" I hissed in her ear while we were playing Monopoly.

"Don't worry, it's a cover for why you don't go with them on their activities. Of course, your father and aunt June knew." She whispered back.

Crime Spree

I was fast asleep when I heard the news reporter on TV stating various robberies and scams and graffiti. I was confused because I couldn't hear anything else and I could tell that it was the TV in the living room. I tried to move, but I was stuck in the same place and the same position.

Finally, he stopped. I was free. I ignored it all morning without telling anyone. At lunch time it happened again. He was reporting more of those types of crimes. I choked on my sandwich and banged my fists on the table. Coco looked up from her newspaper to stare at me.

Cameron took a bite from his sandwich eyeing me with an eyebrow raised. I ignored them and tried to forget what I heard but it just gave me a headache.

At bedtime, I popped cotton buds in my ears and put sweat bands on my limbs. I felt as though I would turn invisible because of the pain but I could control when I did and didn't. I forced myself to sleep that night. I heard the same kind of thing in the morning.

During the day, after walking Lucky, I heard Coco talking about what she read in the newspapers and it was the same thing, I spent the rest of the day making up ways for it to stop. I fell asleep, on my desk, still working.

I was woken the next day by Cameron playing music in my ears.

He made me pancakes and Coco set up fun things for us to do during the day.

We played board games, went to the park, Cameron bought us ice creams, and took Lucky for a second walk. When we got back home, mum asked me to join her outside because we had to learn my special attack for something that was happening tomorrow.

I did as she asked even though I was so confused.

We spent hours trying different ways to attack the dummy

using my powers. I tried confusion, I had to be in one place and disappear then reappear behind them and kick them. We tried fast fury: I would turn invisible and strangle the enemy. There were so many others that we tried, but despite me conquering every move, mum said we hadn't found the one I had a connection with. Finally, we did a move called dark side grind. I had to go invisible and roundhouse kick the dummy. Dad made glasses for mum to see me while I went invisible - I guess the smarts my siblings have, come from dad. Mum said that she could see that I was connected with it. Whatever that means. Just then, dad called mum in a hurried voice.

Coco walked out to the garden with her ball. "Let's play sis." She smiled. I raised an eyebrow at her sudden interest in sports. "Sure, let's play." I said.

We played catch and then Lucky got excited and brought out his fetch toy, forcing us to play fetch with him. I was just about to take back the toy when it happened again. I froze as I heard mum outside.

"We'll have to go to Westminster tomorrow because there's

been too many crimes and they are all connected." I heard her admit. I could finally move.

I sprinted to them in the drive. "MUM MY HAYWIRE! IT'S SUPER HEARING!!" I squealed.

Mum's jaw dropped.

"Well, now you know let's eat dinner and get you to bed." Mum said. I nodded.

I went upstairs but I couldn't sleep. Mum was hiding something. This was a milestone in my super power experience. Mum made a fuss about Coco when she made her first robot. She even started a scrapbook about her programming journey. Mum made a scrapbook about Cameron's non- changed grades. She's made a scrapbook about our choir competitions. So something as huge as this for a measly, 'eat dinner and go to bed', means that something was wrong, or right. I don't know. But I was completely sure that there was something going on for her to brush it off. I had no idea what, but I promised myself that I would get to the bottom of it.

I thought that if I did a lot of sneaking around I'd be able to figure out everything and depending on what it was, maybe even alter it.

I thought and thought.

I brainstormed so hard that I fell asleep.

Chapter 4

Westminster Conference

It was 3:23 in the morning when mum woke me up.

"Quietly pack your things, we've got an hour to leave", she whispered once the curtains opened and I was awake. I slowly gathered my stuff into two suitcases and got into a hoodie and jeans.

"Let's go." Mum uttered. We got into the car, and I immediately fell asleep. It was around 6:20 a.m. when I woke up. Mum was parking.

"Come on." She yawned. Once we got our bags, I followed her to a water fountain. Mum rustled around in her handbag and pulled out a red coin. She dipped it in the water, and it turned orange. I felt as though an invisible hook was pulling me from behind my chest.

The water parted and swiftly sucked us inside. We landed into a blue cart with a thud. Mum swiped the coin on the front, and we zoomed towards a bright light. After a roller-coaster-like kind of ride, we arrived in front of a blue and silver door. She squeezed the coin and made me do the same. She tapped it on the keyhole, and it shot another out of it. The door swung open, and mum gave me the second coin.

I looked up at the grand room I was standing in. People were busying around. Mum waved at a woman who looked very important as she waltzed over.

"Lisa! It's been a while!" Mum shrieked, hugging her.

"May! I know that June couldn't join us. But April should be here." Lisa beamed.

"Auntie April's here?" I gasped.

"Oh! You must be Cora!" Lisa cooed. "Yes, your aunt is here somewhere, but you'll need to see something." She chuckled.

"Sebastian, take Miss Cora to the room!" A timid man stepped to her. "Oh, and don't forget to take her bags." Lisa ordered.

He took my things and led me to an archway. There were a thousand white doors with numbers on them.

David directed me to room 406. When he opened the door, I saw a girl listening to music on a bed, another girl in a yoga pose, a boy on his phone and another boy watching the TV.

"Hello children, I have one more child that's staying with you. Cora, this is Olivia, Chloe, Carlos and Luke." He said. "Don't lose this coin; it's your key." He gave me the coin and my bags. I awkwardly waved at the others.

"So, Cora, what can you do?" Sneered the one in a yoga pose. I closed my eyes, and focused on the icy feeling that washed over me.

"Cool!" A boy shrieked.

"Sure, Luke, only if you haven't seen mine." The snob said. She screwed up her eyes, and slowly morphed into a butterfly. "Oh, and I'm Chloe." She squeaked.

"That's nothing!" A boy laughed. He took a glass of water and focused on it. The water floated out of the cup, and he made it go all around the room and ended in a lovely display. "The name's Carlos."

"Look at me!" The girl on the bed yelled. She held out her hand and stared at it. A fire started then she moved it to the TV, and suddenly it stopped. "Olivia." She smiled.

"You call that power?" Luke teased. He stared at my suitcase. "I see cream, shoes, lotion, perfume and an EpiPen." he said, triumphantly.

"Let's see your other bag. Oooh, tops, skirts, tights, leggings, lipstick, lip gloss, eye shadow, blush... Hey what're those?" He pressed invasively. I realised what he was looking at was my teddy bear from when I was a baby. It seems silly, but I thought he was a lucky charm with a sweet little blanket when I was little. I brought him to not feel homesick.

"OK,THAT'S ENOUGH!" I screamed, swinging the bag behind my back. The other girls laughed, and Carlos just stared at us like we were crazy.

"It's just some stuff that only we are allowed to know about." Olivia smiled at Luke.

"Can you two go to your room?" Chloe demanded, staring apologetically at me. Luke made his way next door.

"But Zach's in there", Carlos complained. "Or not." he sighed as a tiny toddler waddled in.

"Cowa!" Zach gurgled, running to me. Zach is my aunt April's 3-year-old son. I picked him up and hoisted him onto my hip.

"You lot can go, we'll watch Zach." Olivia commented, blowing a raspberry on Zach's stomach. The boys left, and we made a fuss over Zach.

"Where are you from?" I asked Chloe.

She waved a hand dismissively. "Finland but I live in Portugal. You?"

"Jamaica but I live here." I answered. "Olivia?"

"Mexico but I live in Croatia." Olivia replied.

"COOL! So can you speak Spanish?" I said.

"Hola, mi nombre es Olivia. And Croatian, Zdravo moje ime je Olivia. Now, Chloe."

"Ugh! Ola meu nome e Chloe."

We giggled and joked about so many different things. Like how once when Olivia asked David what his favourite colour was, he said that he didn't have one because he didn't want to upset the other colours. Then we went out of the room to look for aunt April.

"Awe we gowing to see mummy?" Zach babbled, jumping up and down. I lifted him in the air like a rocket.

"Yes, we are", I replied. We ran to the main hall and pretended that Zach was flying.

"Pilot Zachery, do you see your mum?" Chloe said in a walky-talky voice.

Zach shook his head. That's when I saw my auntie April talking to mum.

"Zach!" Mum exclaimed.

"Plane landing on May's lap. Beep, beep, beep." Olivia murmured as I lowered Zach onto mum's lap.

He cuddled up to her as I hugged aunt April. She asked me about school. I wrinkled my nose in disdain.

"I see it's not very good. Well, you have your super life now. Zach's upset that he won't have any powers like you guys." She filled in for me. I smiled and tickled Zach's stomach. He giggled and flapped his legs in the air. Lisa and David got everyone's attention.

"Hello everyone! We would like to inform you that breakfast is served. Then, you are free to explore. Tomorrow, we adults will be in our meeting while Cora, Chloe, Zach, Olivia, Carlos and Luke can practice their powers in their rooms." Lisa announced.

David led the way to a massive canteen. I sat next to Olivia and made sure that Luke was sitting nowhere near me. I was too embarrassed to even let him see my face. I took some toast and scrambled eggs and drank some orange juice with it too.

I saw mum trail off from the rest of us. Slowly, I noticed that most of the adults were acting really mysterious. I was sure that I could find out what was happening, but I needed to ask some certain people for some help. I took out several napkins and pulled my fountain pen out.

I wrote on it: Tonight at the girl's room. When everyone's asleep, come with ideas and directions to the soundproof conference room. Be stealthy.

I folded the napkins into paper aeroplanes. I threw one at

Chloe, which landed in her hair. She disgustedly took it out. She read it and gave me a thumbs up. I threw one at Carlos, and he did the same. So did Luke. I whispered the plan into Olivia's ear. She mischievously grinned. We spent the entire day watching our parents mingle, and it got awkward really, really fast.

We sat in the lounge, all of us kids sat with our parents, and we were all chatting. Then, the weird bit came. Chloe's mum was bragging about her and how flexible she is because of her shapeshifting. She was a very snobby woman. So I guess Chloe's mean demeanour comes from her mum showing her off. But even though she can seem like a mean, insensitive snob, she's quite caring and sweet underneath it all. She just has to put on a front because her mum is always putting it in her head to be the best.

"Chloe, dear, why don't you show them your gymnastics." Her mum flexed.

"Oh! Cora has been doing that too." Mum said excitedly.

So we got up and Chloe whispered a routine in my ears. We did opposite cartwheels, then round offs in the opposite direction. She did a backbend, and held it while I did an aerial over her. Then all of our parents got defensive, and we ended up being forced to one-up each other, which none of us wanted to do. Chloe did a backflip, so Oliva had to dance for us, and I had to sing, Luke was forced to beatbox, so Carlos had to rap.

It was really uncomfortable. We spent the majority of the day showing off unwillingly. At dinner, we sat next to each other so we could speak about how we felt.

Chloe is always pressured to be the best. Once, her mum glared and shouted at her for losing because she fell and sprained her ankle. Her mum is constantly showing off their money, so she always makes Chloe wear the most expensive things and marinades her face in makeup.

Chloe has been in so many competitions since she was two. Olivia said that she was always tired because she felt as though her family's reputation was high; she would be a shame to them if she didn't keep up. Carlos felt like because he was the eldest sibling he was the example, he was always the strong one, but it's all too much for him.

Luke said that because of the way his family is, he is never allowed to cry or get angry. Well, not unless it's for a reason they find worthy. Because he's always struggling to hide his feelings, sometimes at nights he lays in his bed and silently cries.

They all looked at me to share my feelings. "I'm pressured because all my life I've been competing for attention. Now that my powers have come in early, I have the attention I've craved. But I don't want to lose their attention, so I have to keep making a splash." I sighed.

Tears started to build up in Chloe's eyes, her eyeshadow dripped and so did her eyeliner, and mascara. I took a napkin and wiped her face. I started to cry, and so did Olivia. Soon, all of us were crying.

"Look, as teens, we are under *a lot* of pressure." Carlos sniffed. We made noises of agreement.

"And superpowers are even more on us." Luke wailed.

I dried my eyes and an idea came to my head.

"How about, we make a secret group where we can share our fears and worries or anything that bothers us."

"What about us living in different countries?" Coughed Olivia through her tears. I wiped off her teardrops. "We can video chat anytime!" Exclaimed Chloe, reapplying more makeup before her mum came.

If I were to sum up our issues, I would say that Chloe always has to win, Olivia has a reputation to maintain, Carlos has to stay strong, Luke is never allowed to show emotions, and, I'm in a contest to get attention. We quickly pretended to be laughing about something because our parents came by.

"It's time for bed." Lisa said, softly.

We got out of our seats and pretended to be really tired so that nobody would be suspicious. Olivia, Chloe and I went into our room.

I snuggled under the sheets and made fake snoring noises. "That sounds too much like you're forcing it." Chloe pointed out. I tried even harder to sound natural.

"That's better" she remarked.

I don't think Olivia could hear us because she had her headphones in. She stuck her head under the quilt, but I could still see her shape swaying very slightly. Chloe turned off the lights. After 1 or 2 hours we decided to whisper to each other.

"What's your super haywire?" Olivia whispered.

"Super hearing. You?" I replied under my breath.

" Super speed, Chloe?" she answered quietly.

"Super flexibility", she mumbled.

There were a few more minutes of awkward conversation, but I was done with it so even though I was nowhere near tired, I deflated myself in my bed and waited for the boys to come.

"Why do you want to do this anyway?" asked Olivia. I got a little annoyed because I wanted to be left alone. Luckily, before I had to answer her the boys knocked on the door.

"Come in." Chloe whispered.

The door slowly opened.

"Let's go to the conference room." Carlos whisper-shouted. I could tell that they were about to start talking, and I just wanted to get this done with so I could get answers. Before anyone could say anything, I marched out into the corridor.

"Cora! You can't just walk out there! You'll be caught!" Chloe hissed. I ignored her and went invisible.

"Not all of us can do that, show off!" Olivia said and flipped her hair like she was offended.

I made sure I was back in their sights, gave them the sassiest side-eye I could, flipped my hair mockingly and stomped away with my head held high.

"Come on guys." I heard Luke say around the corner, followed by the sound of footsteps coming around to meet me.

I walked ahead of them as quickly as I could to show that it was my plan, and I was the leader. We turned to the breakroom, and I told Chloe to morph into a fly, slip through the door, tranform into a human again and open the door.

We went inside and sat around the table. I turned on the lights and got us some hot chocolate.

"So this is the plan." I said as I handed out the hot chocolate.

"Luke will be lookout using his powers to see through walls. Olivia will distract the guards by creating a fake fire, Carlos you'll be on standby, just in case something goes wrong with the fire you can put it out. Chloe, you stay with me. Shape-shift into a fly so you won't be spotted and I'll be invisible. Chloe, do your unlock thing and we can sneak in and see."

The anxiety in me built up as they fell silent. I stared at their faces. Once they processed the plan through in their minds they started nodding in approval. We got up and were about to leave when Luke burst out with, "what should our team name be? We need it."

"How about the fantastic five!" Carlos suggested.

"No, the fabulous five!" Olivia cried.

"No way! The flawless five sounds-"

"We'll be Team Super or Super Squad!" I announced. They all made murmurs of agreement. So that was how the Team Super was born. That is where the story really started to un-fold. And this is where I wished that I hadn't chosen this life-style.

Plan in Action

We carried out our plan perfectly until we went into the conference room.

"WHAT?" I screamed as we scanned the empty room. I was sure that something was up. The only reason that I permitted myself to scream was that the room was soundproof, and we had closed the door.

"Let's go Cora." Chloe sighed, opening the door. But I refused to budge. "It was a great plan. We can try it again tomorrow." She said firmly as she grasped my arm and tugged as hard as she could. I gave up and stopped resisting. As we walked, tears rolled down my cheeks.

All this for nothing.

We went back to the rest of the team and told them what happened.

"We can try tomorrow", Luke said quietly after trying to pat me on the back to make me feel better, making me scowl and kick a nearby statue.

We dragged our feet back to our rooms. While they whispered goodbye to each other, I threw myself onto my bed and pulled the covers right up over my head. I spent the night making sure nothing would go wrong tomorrow. I figured, to ensure our plan to work we would have to do more things than just following the program. We would have to also:

1. Steal anything that our parents could use to find us.

2. Keep Chloe up high so nobody can smoosh her.

3. Make everyone think that we're outside.

4. Get communicators.

5. Do it before Zach wakes up.

Something that would be ambitious would be the communicators. Still, I knew that Coco had made ten for some freaky science project and Cameron would be able to send it undetected directly to my room by tomorrow morning. I was sure that Cameron would still be awake so I texted him.

YOU: Cameron?

CAM: What Cora, I'm talking to someone.

YOU: Ooohh, is it your podcast group??

CAM: Not that it bothers you but no.

YOU: ooooooooh are you lying?

CAM: Do you want me or not?

YOU: Yes. So, Please could you get Coco to lend me five of her communicator thingies?? Please.

CAM: What's in it for me??

YOU: ...Umm They've got some crazy joke candies.

CAM: And?

YOU: And... They have your favourite sweets.

CAM: What? The sour worms?

YOU: Yes!!

CAM: And for Coco???

YOU: She can wear my favourite pearl bracelet while I'm away!!!

Does this mean you'll do it??

CAM: It depends...

YOU: ANYTHING

CAM: Stop bugging my friends when they come over...

ESPECIALLY the others at the podcast.

YOU: Just them? Pleeeease?

CAM: Not Joking Cora.

YOU: FINE!!!

CAM: They'll be there tomorrow without anyone noticing. What

room number are you?

YOU: 406. THANKS CAMERON!!!!

CAM: Don't forget the deal.

So that was that. I fell asleep ready to explain everything
to Team Super.

I woke up to the girls' shocked gasps. I immediately un-
derstood why they were so shocked. I sat bolt upwards, and
my eyes snapped open. "DON'T TOUCH THE PACKAGE!" I bellowed. They jumped at my sudden outburst.

"Oh, good, you're awake." Chloe snarled. I ignored her and leant over my bed to pick up the box. There was a note attached to it. Which read:

Cora, send the sweets and bracelet through this. If the guards find it they will let it slide if you say you miss us and want to send us a care package.

-Cameron & Coco

I tore open the box, and in a plastic container, there were five earpieces.

"What even are those?" Gawped Olivia, staring at the box. I held the plastic container as if it was the most precious diamond in the world.

"These are a part of a new plan that I devised last night." I grinned. "So, get dressed, and we can go to the breakroom." I beamed. Chloe was just about to protest when Olivia jabbed her in the ribs to keep her quiet.

They ran into our enormous bathroom; there were three mirrors, three sinks and three toilets. We even had three showers and one bath.

Everything seemed covered in sparkly glass. Wherever you looked, there was either golden glitter, shiny silver glass or glistening diamantes. We brushed our teeth, showered, combed our hair and got dressed. We decided to all wear a yellow top and denim jeans to show that it was a team uniform, though my top had a picture of animals on the front, Olivia's had flowers and Chloe was wearing a crop top.

I took the box, and we walked to room 405. We knew the boys wouldn't be awake at this time because the first day we knocked on their door, it took an hour for them to wake up. So, Chloe did her favourite door unlocking trick, and we crept into their room.

We picked clothes for them that matched our 'uniform' and set it quietly on their beds. I looked into Zach's crib and saw him curled up, sucking his thumb, sleeping peacefully. I scooped him up and took him outside. We didn't want to wake him when we made the noise to wake the boys.

I could hear the girls were making an effort to make as much noise as possible. They made bangs, clangs, booms, clashes and some noises that were most likely them straight out screaming. After a little while of making noise, the door opened, "they'll be out in a second." Chloe said triumphantly. Once the boys were ready, and Zach was back in his crib, we set off for the breakroom. This time though, we had to keep our voices down because people were walking around. I told them everything. I didn't really care what they thought because it was the only way we would get any answers. While they were chatting about the pros and cons of my plan, I took the joke candies, the gummy worms and my bracelet. I put it in the box and ran up to Lisa.

"Hi Cora. What's wrong?"

"Nothing, it's just that I want to send this parcel of sweets to my big brother and this pearl bracelet to my little sister. But, I'm not sure how to send it." I said in my cutest voice, batting my eyelashes.

Lisa took the parcel, smiling and carried it away.

I returned to the group. I stared at them, waiting for them to tell me if they were in or not.

"So, what're we waiting for? Let's get out there and get

answers then!" Oliva exclaimed. We group hugged and set out for victory, putting our plan into motion.

Phase one: steal any disadvantages.

I described my Mum's glasses she used to see me with to them so they could hide them while I distracted the parents. I knew that they all loved coffee and was convinced that they barely slept last night. I decided to make the best coffee I could to distract them. I spread the word that I was making coffee so that they watched me make it.

I was very uncomfortable with this, but I had to distract them for as long as humanly possible. I put it in the fancy cups so that they couldn't leave from the table until they had completely finished. Just as the most boring conversation happened, Carlos was signalling for me to finish up and go. I ran from the table and followed them down the hallway.

Phase 2: stations.

Chloe turned into a fly, and I turned invisible. The others ran to the posts where the guards were located and started to work their magic.

Chloe navigated herself to the ceiling and wove in and out of lampshades, I had the harder job of silently navigating in and out of people.

Finally, we got there and ran into the room. I climbed up onto a shelf and turned on the earpiece so that the team could hear every word. Lisa sat at the front of the huge room at a table. Sebastian sat behind her, with his back to the room.

I decided to risk it and climb down to try and steal a glimpse of what he was doing that Lisa seemed unaware of and seemed like it would be terrible for him if anyone saw it. I chose to just take a sneak peek, climbing down as quietly as I could, I made my way across to where he was sitting.

I was halfway there when adults started filling the room. I almost bumped into someone, so I got scared and made a break for it. I hoisted myself onto an unoccupied table and jumped from that to the lining of the curtains.

I crawled into an empty cabinet. I'm still not sure how I did it, but it felt as if I blinked and I just ended up on it.

They say that fear makes you do crazy things. I felt my leg getting a cramp and started getting impatient. Who could blame me? I mean, I was stuck in a cabinet, in an awful position, waiting for answers. It was terrible!

Eventually, Lisa started talking. I listened intently. "We know that there is a mole in the agency. Now, here's the thing that mole is working for the HEAD of crime. This person wants control over all magic in the world, even extra-terrestrial. We need a team to be trained by our finest warriors. I have been informed that our children have better chances of being the ones trained."

My jaw dropped.

I couldn't do that!

Last month I was trying to not fail miserably at a backflip! Now I'll be facing the head of crime! In an agency? With a mole? No way! I was NOT consulted! Besides, I hate the pressure of school plays. There is no way in the entire galaxy that I would be able to handle the pressure of saving the world from danger.

I mean keeping it all a secret AND going to school AND continue training! I almost fainted. I couldn't even believe it! Imagine what could happen if I made one stupid childish mistake. I could die, or worse, put my family in danger, or, worst of all, letting the world down!

"I know what you're all thinking, but he doesn't know the strengths and weaknesses of these kids. Everyone sitting here has faced him, even me. So, parents of these children get ready."

Parents get ready? What about the kids who have no clue about anything? Well, no clue about it if we were doing what we were supposed to be doing. I saw a hand rise. "I'm sorry, but I've got to get Zach all ready", said a voice that I recognised as auntie April's.

At these words, I jumped up. I opened the door of the cabinet and jumped around frantically. The door was closed, and they would notice if I opened it. I ran to the window and slowly opened it.

"What are you doing?" Chloe hissed into the earpiece. I kept my mouth shut because I was very close to a table filled with people. I climbed onto the window sill and jumped down. I was finally outside. In a panic, I looked around and auntie April was already gone! I let myself drift back into sight and searched hurriedly for a window that led to our room.

Chloe came out of the window and turned back into herself. "Come on. I know where our window is! It's the one over there. But we'll have to cover up our clothes with our bedsheets", she instructed. As she unlocked the window with her key, I yelled, "Abort, Abort! Get into your rooms now and hide your clothes!" into the communicator.

When Chloe had finally opened the window, I rushed through it and luckily, I landed on my bed. I kicked off my shoes and hid under the covers. Chloe scrambled to her bed, and Olivia dashed into the room. "The door!!" Chloe and I shouted at her. She ran back, slammed the door and slid under the covers.

"Can you believe how easy that was?" Olivia panted.

"That wasn't easy! Did you see what I had to do?" I puffed.

"Yes, but it wasn't hard, we didn't even get caught", Chloe

replied in a voice that indicated that she was deep in thought. I was about to speak, but auntie April came in, holding a talkative Zach.

"Wakey-wakey girls." She called. I wasn't sure what to do next. We were done for! I slid into my dressing gown. Even though I couldn't put my nightshirt on, I slid it through the dressing gown so it looked like I was wearing it. I sat up and smiled, "good morning auntie." Zach came to hug me and sat on my lap.

"Wake up your friends for me please." She chirped. She left the room, and I took off the dressing gown. "She's gone." I whispered. The girls sat up and Olivia started walking to the door.

"What're you doing?" Chloe sighed.

"Getting the boys so we can go to the cafe around the corner and explore," she said as if it was a stupid question to ask. Chloe got up and followed her.

"Aren't you coming?" Olivia asked, staring me up and down.

It took a while for me to realise what she was thinking.

"I'm not trying to go back to the conference room. I'm getting Zach ready. I might take him toy shopping." I giggled at her.

"Ok but, in 10 minutes you should be on your way." Chloe said, staring at me. I waved a dismissive hand. They left the room and I heard them banging on the door next to us.

"Ok, Zach do you want a superman T-shirt with jeans or a spiderman top with trousers?" I wondered aloud.

Zach pointed to his baby bag and squealed, "Spiderman! Marvel! Marvel!" clapping his hand happily. So I put him in a spiderman top and blue trousers. We went to the cafe and had the most delectable croissants I've ever tasted, finished off with some amazing scones. Suddenly something crisp went up my nose.

"Do you smell that?" Luke asked, standing up. Everyone took suspicious sniffs of the air. "Yeah, it smells like -" But Chloe was cut off because someone was screaming at the top of their lungs that there was a fire.

"We've got to help them!" Olivia shrieked. We all got ready to pounce into action, but Chloe looked at us like we were crazy. "Are you mad? We can't do that! We're just little kids! There is nothing we can do about it, we're only kids. Cora, you're with me, right?"

"Well you're right about one thing, we are kids. But we're kids with superpowers! We can do this if we do more than our best because failure isn't even a question." I replied.

"SUPER SQUAD!" We cheered.

"Olivia, try to make sure nobody gets burned, Carlos, put out as much fire as possible, Chloe, turn into something that flies and can carry people and I'll try to keep the building up", I instructed. The team scattered, and I watched them jump and dodge flaming bits off the building that fell towards them. I felt useless. I hated it.

I spent most of my time worrying, and I didn't notice the building falling towards me. Everyone was out and behind me. I was petrified. I tried to run, but my feet couldn't move, I did whatever I could to move, but all I could do was put my arms in front of my body, I felt so stupid.

Something rose in my stomach. It burst out of my hands and I was almost knocked off my feet. I had no idea where this energy blast came from. I forced my eyes open and saw that a purple bubble coming from my hands had formed around the building, holding it up.

The team stared at me with their jaws to the floor. I shrugged and tried to keep myself strong. I saw a black figure floating in mid-air. I stared at it, wondering what it could be when my vision became blurred.

It whizzed away, and I could feel all my energy draining from me as if someone had just got a vacuum and sucked it out. I knew that I couldn't hold it up much longer, but I pushed my energy for as long as it could hold. The team must have taken a hint because Olivia ran over to me to help me stay on my feet, Chloe turned into a cheetah to try and take objects to barricade the building, Luke called our parents and Carlos called the police. Before I knew it, I couldn't stand up for much longer. The last thing I remembered seeing before I blanked out was Olivia checking on me and people filming.

After that, all I can remember was darkness.

Chapter
6

Getting in Gear

I heard sirens and people talking with my name in their conversation. I slowly opened my eyes. I was in a bed, but I didn't recognise where. It was plain and simple. I sat up, and around me were light pink walls with animal stickers in the most random places.

"Look, she's alright!" Someone said. I looked up to see a brunette haired lady staring at me with warm blue eyes, and a wide smile.

"You must be Olivia's mum." I croaked, staring at her sporty clothes and sweatband on her head. She hugged me and called someone's name. A girl looked at me and waved. "This is Nicole and Nicholas," Olivia's mum smiled motioning to the girl.

"NICHOLAS! Get over here!" she yelled at the boy who was playing on the curtains as if it were monkey bars. He jumped down to say hello.

"Where am I?" I asked.

"You are in the children's hospital ward." A lady said, looking down at me, in a leopard print jacket, fancy pearl sunglasses, snakeskin purse and a Beverly Hills haircut. She was definitely Chloe's mum. I mean her name was Kendall. I got up, but Nicole picked me up and hoisted me back into the bed. After a while, they left, and mum entered the room.

"Can I please go home now?" I groaned.

"No, Cora. We still have to get you into training and super suited up." She abruptly answered as she scrolled through her phone.

"Wait. T-t-training?, W-what?"

"Don't play dumb with me Cora. I'm fully aware of what happened. When I saw that the glasses weren't in my hand-bag, I knew that you were up to something." Mum cut me off.

"You're telling me that a group of thirteen and four-teen-years old were dumb enough to steal directly from your handbag." I moaned.

"Oh yes and they left my room in a mess after raiding it", she said, rolling her eyes.

I hid my face in my pillow.

"But the point is that you're going and you're going now", she responded firmly.

I got out of the bed and glowered. I followed mum out of the hospital and once we got into the hotel, I bolted up the stairs. She ran behind me and I wouldn't let her catch me. More of the fact that she would kill me if she got me. I saw a room, and leapt into it. I tried to climb the shelves, but I felt mum's hands grip me from behind. She tugged me off them and carried me down the stairs and into a fancy room.

I screamed and squirmed, shouted and pushed. I even bit her, but she never gave up. All of Team Super was there, staring at me with wide eyes. I blushed and waited for mum to put me down. "May we never speak of this again." I said, staring at all of them. They all nodded slowly, still confused. I brushed myself off and waited for the person that Lisa had described.

Crystal came in, followed by Olivia's mum. Chloe and Olivia groaned and slumped in their chairs. Crystal sat daintily in the chair, and when Olivia's mum threw herself into her chair, and banged a box onto the round table, she barked, "I'm Monica and this is Crystal. We are the ones who will be doing your suits. I'll be sewing it and Crystal here will design."

We spent a few hours there, and before I knew it, we were being ushered out towards another door. It was a huge room with assault courses, stations, and an empty space. A woman with a stern expression marched into the vacant space and another with a smile skipped next to her. "I'm Zarah, and she's Ally. We are the best warriors that Superheroes around the globe can offer. We will train you to be the best you that you can be." Explained the one that was smiling. "Let's get started!"

She led us to the assault course, pushing Olivia onto the first step, and pressed a few buttons. The course sprang to life, and a stopwatch was pushed into my hands. I pressed it the minute Olivia took her first dodge. After around six tries she did a two miles long assault course in under five minutes.

She had several bruises and three cuts all over herself.

By the time I went, it was dark, and everyone else was visibly injured. I gulped and started. The first stage was flexibility. Spiky bats flew across, and spikes pointed through the floor; I had special shoes on so the spikes wouldn't hurt, but I still couldn't crawl beneath them. I had to bend backwards as far as I could without touching the floor.

I walked towards the second stage, but before I even got past the second bat, something sharp stabbed my side, and I was shoved off. I fell to the floor and rolled towards Ally's feet. She muttered something about us being weak. I decided to prove her wrong. I went back and tried again. I was poked in my side. I almost fell but stood up straight and turned around. Flattening myself, I wove in and out. Then I had to get through smoke, speed.

Then I was followed by Ally and found a way to lose her, wits. After that, I had to get past a rigged rock climbing station, resilience. Next, I had to dodge a laser security system, agility.

Once we were done, she sent us to our rooms when I had finished. Even though I had scratches, bruises and cuts all over me, I only fell off once. I didn't care though. I refused to use those skills as I would not face the Master of Crime and Evil. That was what I thought until Ally called me.

"You are promising Cora, don't let fear deprive you of your potential. I started this when I was a teenager, a little older than you and not only did I not have the support you have, but I also hadn't had my powers yet." She looked at me as she spoke. "Do you think I didn't have any doubts? I got through them with an amazing mentor, your cousin. I'll be that person to you by giving you this." I reached out to take it from her. "Oh, don't touch it yet. This is a very special ring." She said to me.

I nodded, taking note of the fact that it must be very valuable. I cautiously opened the badly wrapped present. It was beautiful. "That was your ancestor Helen's ring. She gave it up when the group gave up their prized possession for the word's safety." Ally grinned, watching me turn the ring around. I was very surprised that Ally was capable of being so thoughtful and caring, especially towards a 'weakling' like myself. I took it gratefully and made my way to the canteen for dinner.

Even though it felt like my limbs were going to fall off, I was the tiniest bit happy. I gulped my food and hurried to our bedroom. The other girls followed me to see what I was up to but fell asleep.

I texted Coco. You might think that Coco would be unsafe with a phone because she's only seven, but she's safer and can be trusted more with that thing than Cameron and I.

YOU: Hi Coco beans

COCO BEANS: Greetings

YOU: What child says greetings?

COCO BEANS: Me, I miss you :(

YOU: Me too

COCO BEANS: When will you be back

YOU: Not till summer's over, sorry little sis

COCO BEANS: But you've been dancing since summer started! I want to spend the holiday with u

YOU: I know. Now, I have a mystery for you.

COCO BEANS: YEEEESSS???

YOU: Do you know anything about Helen's ring

COCO BEANS: Don't play with my emotions!!

YOU: I'm not, do you have a lead.

COCO BEANS: NO :)

YOU: You'd have to do so much research then and dad will be at work and aunt June is well, here.

COCO BEANS: Exactly!! I'll get to read up on lab stuff

YOU: I really don't understand how I was eating my hair when I was your age and you read science books from a labs' library about heritage.

COCO BEANS: Sorry, I couldn't hear you over the sound of my brain working. Could you complement me again and text my praises?

YOU: No.

COCO BEANS: Whatever.

Hero Lessons

I woke up to the worst alarm clock ever!

"GET UP YOU LOT! RISE AND SHINE MAGGOTS!" Ally cried. She shone the brightest flashlight on the planet in our faces.

"AAAAAAAHHHH!" I shrieked, jumping up and putting up my fists. "Are we under attack?" I hyperventilated.

"Nope, just our coaches." Carlos yawned from the door.

"GO, GO, GO!" Zarah shouted. We ran in a straight line to the canteen - though we were still in our pyjamas. Once we were served the slop Zarah called 'nutritious stew', that I hardly believe was made for human consumption, we were led to the design room which had our super costumes.

We got changed and jogged around the building.

Ally's long black hair flowed from behind her, and her ear-piercing shimmered from behind her ear. Zarah's curly blonde hair billowed out from behind her. As she ran, it bounced up and down, while us kids probably looked constipated.

Once we got back into the training room, Ally took us to a table. "Luke, let's work on you first." she grinned, knowing that we would most likely hate the upcoming lesson. Luke looked taken aback and gulped. "I'm going to help you push your powers to the limit and let you all do things you never knew you could." She continued.

She gestured for him to stand. As he did, we watched him intently. "Now, I'm going to help you get to a stage where you can read minds. Olivia, you will be able to create warm temperatures, cold for Carlos. Chloe, my princess, you will turn into anything, not just animals you've seen. But anything. As for you, Miss Martin, you will be able to not only create force fields but levitate things and bend to your whim." Her explanation was met by silence from us.

Luke stepped into a contraption. When Ally turned it on his face went blank, as if he couldn't see any of us and had no sense of reality. After a few seconds, he started struggling and yelping as if he was in great pain.

Ally pushed me into one. I tried to run, but she already pressed the 'on' button. I was transported to another dimension. Everything around was glowing. I saw someone or rather, something sinister. It looked evil, and I saw it creeping towards my family. It pounced onto them. Then something arose inside of me. I had never felt like that before. Suddenly the creature emerged in the air. I wanted to make it hurt. Extremely hurt. And it was!

It twisted around in the air, and then it saw me. It dropped onto the floor and charged at me. I tried to turn invisible, but I had no idea if it had worked or not. The shadowy figure ignored me and tried to go after my family again. This time I wouldn't let it. I tried to focus on the icy feeling and sent my anger at it. The thing ascended into the air again, and it's body twisted into painful shapes.

My body surged with pain, but I didn't care. "LEAVE THEM ALONE!" I bellowed before being shot back into reality. Luke and Chloe were already back, both looking tired. I crumbled to the floor. When Carlos came back at the same time as Olivia, Zarah took us out for lunch.

"All of that stuff you went through today, and the things that happened to the thing you faced, it was all you." Zarah beamed, guzzling her drink.

I almost choked on my burger. Olivia, ignoring the work ethics started laughing very hard at me as I still struggled to stop coughing and spluttering. "What child even eats a plate of salad for lunch when given a choice?" Carlos raised an eyebrow at Chloe, making us all laugh.

"What child eats wasabi on noodles?" She shot back.

They stared at each other for a while before Luke intercepted and drove the conversation towards our super costumes. Don't worry, we changed into normal clothes, so we didn't look crazy in public. Ally came to ruin our fun though.

"Come on, time to do it in reality without power enhancers", she said sternly, met by a series of groans. We were marched back to the dreaded room. I sat sulkily on a chair that had my name on it. In front of me was a big pole.

I was told to wait in silence until Ally and Zarah came to me. While I watched them, they taught Chloe to turn into a centaur, Luke to tell everyone in the room what I was thinking about, Olivia to create a dull heat and Carlos to drench Ally in icy cold water. "Hello Miss Ally." I snickered as she approached me. "Are you thirsty, I can get you some water." I giggled. I saw Zarah's mouth twitch upwards, and she struggled to control her chuckles. A snort slipped out of her mouth, and none of us could contain it anymore. We burst into laughter to the point where some of us were crying and the rest were coughing uncontrollably. While Ally's face remained stony and unimpressed.

"Are we finished here?" Ally grunted. We burst out into fresh fits of giggles. Zarah, trying to compose herself, slammed her fist down on her desk, making an ink bottle fly into Ally's face. She looked like a badger in a bad mood.

"You have a little something on your face ma'am." I said in a genuine voice. Everyone started wheezing with laughter. "Ha. Ha. Ha. I see you might be quite the class clown. Let's see if your grades are any better than your jokes, and for your sake, hope they are way *way* better." Ally replied coldly. "Now Miss Martin, simply pick up the pole with your levitation." She continued.

I squeezed my energy into my palms and pushed it out with all my might -a purple bubble formed around it. The only word I focused on was 'up' and when the pole feebly came off the ground, I lifted my hands high above the air, and the pole followed it. I gave Ally the greatest look of triumph ever and just to prove something to her; I flew it around the room. "Great, now turn it into a circle." she grinned, knowing that I couldn't do that. I gawped at her, unable to believe that she expected a thirteen-year-old to manipulate a pole.

"It is merely foam, Martin." Ally smiled smugly. After what I'm guessing was two minutes of humiliation I had pretty much given up. But when I saw Ally's intent, eyes watching me and her snide smile, I was determined to get the last laugh. I started to move my hands into a circle. I tried to bring them close together, riding on my determination and finally on the last circular motion the pole was bent into a spiral pattern. "I do not remember telling you to put it to a spiral.

Just a simple circle." She spoke in a tone that showed how bitter she was as I went above expectations.

I decided to make the pole unravel and follow her around and whack her. "YOU- STOP- THAT - RIGHT- NOW!" Ally yelled, dodging the pole. I tried making it seem as though I couldn't help it and made the pole shoot in her direction. It flew towards her as a boulder shot out of a canon. She froze for a few seconds then bolted out of the room.

Oh, how I regret that.

Over the next few weeks, she was tough on us and even harder on me. But the one day that really changed me was the last day before heading out to fight. I was expecting lots of labour, but when we walked in, there was a table and Ally was sitting there with Zarah, and they both looked serious.

"Before we let you go we're just going to put you in a simulator to show you what your jobs are. You know, our drone flyers." Said Zarah. For the first time, she sounded mournful. We gave each other worried looks and stepped into the mini room. I saw a seat with my name on it and a desk with loads of computers. I turned over the label, and it said: **right wing protector**.

"I'm pilot!" gasped Olivia.

"And I'm co-pilot." remarked Luke. They looked at each other for a long time as if they were silently having a conversation.

"Alright, uhh, who's right wing protector?" Chloe asked, searching around. I waved at her without looking up from the computers.

"I'm left." She smiled.

"I'm an engine protector." Carlos muttered. We took our seats and started typing. Finally the room started to shake and the windows faded into an image of the sky. Unfortunately, I couldn't get the hang of the quick typing and neither could Chloe. At first, we lost our wings, and on our second try, we lost our engine. On our third try, we went the wrong way. But on our fourth try, we got there perfectly, and we just passed the villains with a few hard blows.

"You can come out now, team." Came Ally's voice from the speaker. We trudged to the other room where blue costumes were waiting for us.

"Get changed." Zarah instructed. Once I had looked in the mirror when in costume, I almost screamed. It was great! It was a green latex jumpsuit covering my hands and heels, it had a blue S in a swirl, and next to it was a small blue T.

We went back into the rooms and were attacked by hair artists who were carelessly ripping out my plaits and roughly brushed my hair. They put my hair into a tight, high ponytail. They shoved a bow into my hair and then quickly scurried off.

I looked at the other girls, and they looked the same. The boys wore the same uniform but without anything special for their hair. Ally and Zarah led us towards a place where a huge drone was parked and stood beside Lisa.

As we were about to get water and snacks, our parents launched themselves onto us.

I couldn't exactly hear what Mum was saying due to other parents screaming and wailing. I'm guessing that she said something like: I love you, good luck, but I'm not really sure. Then our parents were taken away from us, and we got hauled off into the drone. I felt a massive lump form in my throat as I took my seat.

"L-let's g-g-get o-out there." Olivia stuttered. We slowly drifted into the air. We went steady until we hit very, very bad turbulence. I started smashing the buttons on the keyboard in a panicky way.

"We'll be there in an hour!" called Luke.

"But we have to go quickly because we're losing power in our wings." Chloe cried.

We jolted, then sped through the air, and my computer started flashing red. This made me hit the buttons even harder and even faster. "WE'VE LOST OUR RIGHT WING!" I yelled, going crazy.

"We have to go faster!" Carlos shouted.

"That's too risky!" Chloe and I answered.

"Olivia, it's your call." sighed Luke.

"I say...it's worth a shot," Olivia replied in a grim voice.

I took a deep breath and waited for the speed.

We started going dangerously fast.

The air pressure started to break the drone.

"WE JUST LOST OUR LEFT WING!" shrieked Chloe. I forced down an anxiety attack and picked up my phone in case we needed help.

"OUR ENGINE IS GONE! I MEAN LITERALLY! KAPUT! IT FELL OUT!" Carlos hollered.

We all started screaming as the drone began falling. I managed to catch a glimpse of Olivia's radar which said that we were close to the lair.

Suddenly, we crashed to the ground, and almost everything shattered. "FIRE!" I screamed. We all dashed to the door and pulled it open. Having bolted away, we watched as the flames destroy the drone.

"Carlos, put it out!" Olivia coughed. Carlos strained, but he did it. Water burst out of his fingers.

We almost made it, but something came from the forest behind us and threw something our way. Smoke emerged from it, and I got sleepier and sleepier. Eventually, I couldn't fight it anymore and gave in.

I fell backwards onto the floor, and the minute I hit the grass, my eyes closed. Though I wasn't comfortable, I still slept easily. And it went black.

Go Team Super

The first thing I remember before waking up, was hearing voices. Were they trying to wake me up? No, they were bickering? Arguing. I don't actually know, but it woke me up either way. It seemed like I was the last person to wake up. My vision came back into focus and I saw that they were all tied to wheelchairs and being driven by aggravated adults in black suits. I tried quickly to levitate the ropes off of us but the person driving me slapped me out of concentration. They drove us deeper and deeper into the forest. "Where's the passcode?" Asked the woman driving Carlos. The others shrugged and fumbled around. "Jack, you bumbling fool! You were supposed to have it!" Snarled the woman pushing me. The others stared accusingly at the man with Olivia. "Hey, I gave it to Sebastian." Jack retorted.

Sebastian, I remember that name! Wait isn't that the name of the receptionist at the conference? I swung my head to see who he was talking about. He took off his sunglasses and put them on Chloe's lap. IT WAS HIM! "No Jack, you gave it to Selena."

Then they all started shouting and then I had a brainwave. **"Annoy them so they don't notice it when Chloe turns into a snake and slithers under the rope to untie us. Stay down when you're untied until we are all free."** Came Luke's voice in my head.

I smiled and nodded then started screaming at the top of my lungs. "Hey kid stop it!" One of them growled. But I only screamed louder and more persistently. Then everyone joined in and some were yelling, others were making animal noises and the rest were whining. Soon all the agents started shouting and begging. Chloe morphed into a snake and fell through the rope. She blended into the grass for a while and then I felt the strain ease. I waited until Chloe turned back into herself and then we all leaped into the air. "GET THEM!" Barked Sebastian.

I dove behind a tree, turned invisible and ran to join the fight. One was headed for Olivia so I punched him in the back of his head. I saw Olivia run towards Jack and set his trousers on fire. When someone tried to help them, Chloe turned into a bull and charged at them. Luke forced two of them to start helping us in the fight. Then when they were all weak, we grabbed the ropes and tied them together. I heard more agents trying to come out of the forest. I quickly turned us all invisible, picked up my phone and levitated us out of the forest.

In no time I called Mum, keeping my voice down. "HEY SWEETPEA!" She shouted.

"Hi Mum." I whispered.

"Oh no, what's wrong?" Gulped Mum, lowering her voice.

"We've crash landed and Sebastian's turned against us. Oh yeah, and we fought adults and won but now more are coming after us." I explained. Mum immediately hung up and I got a cold shiver down my spine. I tuned in my supersonic hearing and heard footsteps. "Guys, let's go." I said under my breath.

I led them to a bush and we crouched behind it. We stayed back there for a few minutes but I saw one of them right behind Chloe. She turned around and let out an ear piercing shriek and started kicking him in the gut. He turned back to her and was just about to pounce when there was a flash of light and Mum appeared in front of us and pushed him into a tree. She headed off to the woods with us following her. Zach was hiding, auntie April was using her earth powers to whack them with vines, aunt June was flying effortlessly and led them into each other, banging their heads.

"The trouble triplets have still got it!" Grinned Mum. Lisa's Limousine parked up and we started filing into it. Zach was almost there when someone grabbed him and started shaking him as bait. If they wanted bait, then bait is what they'll get. I rushed towards them and kicked the woman. She doubled over and dropped Zach.

"RUN!" I insisted. He hurried into the car, I used my protective field around the person rose her into the air and flew her far away. Then, when she was super high, I dropped her.

I couldn't see what happened to her, but I knew that she learnt her lesson. I triumphantly skipped to Lisa's ride and we zoomed away.

A Worthy Award

"Wait, this isn't the way back!" Luke remarked.

"I know. You guys have been nominated by passersby to get badges." Aunt June replied. We made noises of approval and nodded our heads. After a long time, we arrived in front of a tall, fancy building and the inside was even fancier. Mum took me into a corridor with my eyes closed and when she let me open them again, I saw Cameron beaming at me, Coco waving at me and Dad tearing up. They were all holding presents that read how proud they were of me. I didn't know who to hug first! So, I went for them all at the same time. Coco wanted me to open her present first, it was a beautiful necklace with a sapphire in the middle carved into the word Cora. I gave her a kiss on the cheek and then opened Cameron's present which was a set of matching sapphire earrings.

I gave him a huge hug and wouldn't let go until he said, "You have 3 seconds to get off me." I instantly came off of him and got Dad's. It was a lanyard to the VIP section of hair and makeup, "Oh thank you Dad!" I screamed.

"Come on, you're getting a new dress, hair, makeup and access to the backstage area." Mum smiled, ushering me to another corridor. "Hold on, backstage?" I gulped, stopping in my tracks. I had already faced sixteen villains, undertook several brutal trainings, survived a drone crash AND done it all with a concussion. I did NOT need a thousand cameras being stuffed in my face. Mum just laughed and led me into another room where there was a mirror with light bulbs around it. A group of snobby looking women swarmed me. First, they tore my super suit off and replaced it with a chiffon dress but I couldn't see what it looked like because they were busying themselves with my dress. One of them pulled on something on my back, making me hyperventilate. Eventually, they let go and I could breathe again. But as soon as they let me go, they pushed me into the chair and pulled the hair bands out.

They brushed my hair and pulled it about. They swung me around and mobbed me with makeup. Finally, they pushed gloves onto my hands, clipped in my earrings and put on my necklace. A few of them picked me up, then two others put silver heels on me. When they put me down, they pushed me to a mirror and waited excitedly for my reaction. I almost didn't recognise my reflection! I was in a beautiful blue chiffon pencil dress with silver silk gloves and my hair was in a back knot. I loved my new look!

They took me to the backstage area. The others were behind curtains so that we couldn't see each other until the big reveal. The curtains opened and the cameras zoomed in. Olivia covered her mouth in disbelief. Then she saw Luke and he saw her. They stared at each other with their mouths hanging open. Olivia wore a pink satin dress that was around knee high and their hair was in a top spiral leading into a ponytail. Luke wore a grey suit and his hair was slicked back.

Chloe was giggling about it with me and Carlos waved at her. When they saw each other properly, they almost melted.

Chloe was in a velvet, flowy dress and her hair was down. She had an amazing smoky eye, that she did all by herself. Carlos was in a smart tuxedo and his hair was in a big puff. I'm not even going to lie WE. LOOKED. BRILLIANT!

The host started talking and the cameras went away from us, panning over onto the stage. My hands started sweating, my heart was pounding and my stomach was invaded by a swarm of butterflies.

"PLEASE WELCOME CORA MARTIN!" The host yelled into the mic. The crew members motioned for me to go onto the stage. I quickly walked towards the curtains and the second the spotlight fell on me, I froze. Somehow I overcame the feeling of dread and walked to the podium. The host gave me a certificate that read: COMMUNITY HELPER.

I plastered on a fake smile and waved at everyone. Before I knew it Team Super was there with me, waving at the crowd. I was so excited when they let us go backstage again. Don't get me wrong, I'm grateful for the recognition, but I just don't like the whole camera thing.

After a few hours, our parents bustled in. They made us

change into some casual clothes and sit back in Lisa's limousine. She whisked us away and pulled up in front of the airport. "NOOO!" screeched Olivia. "I don't want to go home!" She whined. We gasped and started complaining. "I'm sorry, but we have to go home." sighed Chloe's Mum. We all started crying and hugging. I hated seeing my team go, but I had to. They had lives to get back to. I waved them goodbye, with tears in my eyes and told myself that I'd see them again.

About the Author

Rhae'nell Allen lived in West London and moved to Milton Keynes at age 9. She has always been interested in books and by the time she could write, she started writing short stories.

At the age of 8, with the inspiration from a series of super-hero books she read, she told her parents she wanted to be an author. With their support, she created a relatable character for pre-teens/young teens, in the hope that they too will be inspired by her fictional character and for them to know that they can achieve anything they put their minds to. When she is not writing, she spends her time listening to music, drawing and playing games.

CPSIA information can be obtained
at www.ICGtesting.com
Printed in the USA
BVHW071356060521
606648BV00002B/397